To my Camille, who never gets bored
—M. P.

To my mother, who opened my eyes to the world
—M. D.

Published by
Princeton Architectural Press
202 Warren Street
Hudson, New York 12534
www.papress.com

First edition 2018
© Text: Mathieu Pierloot
© Illustrations: Maria Dek
Published with the permission of Comme des géants inc.,
38, rue Sainte-Anne, Varennes, Québec, Canada J3X1R5
All rights reserved.
Translation rights arranged through the VeroK Agency, Barcelona, Spain

English edition © 2019 Princeton Architectural Press
All rights reserved.
Printed and bound in China by C & C Offset Printing Co., Ltd.
22 21 20 19 4 3 2 1 First edition

ISBN 978-1-61689-828-1

This book was illustrated using watercolors.

For Princeton Architectural Press
Editor: Linda Lee
Typesetting: Paula Baver

Special thanks to: Janet Behning, Abby Bussel, Jan Cigliano Hartman,
Susan Hershberg, Kristen Hewitt, Stephanie Holstein, Lia Hunt, Valerie Kamen,
Cooper Lippert, Jennifer Lippert, Sara McKay, Parker Menzimer, Wes Seeley,
Rob Shaeffer, Sara Stemen, Jessica Tackett, Marisa Tesoro, Paul Wagner,
and Joseph Weston of Princeton Architectural Press
—Kevin C. Lippert, publisher

Library of Congress Cataloging-in-Publication Data available upon request.

LOOK, IT'S RAINING

Mathieu Pierloot

ILLUSTRATIONS BY

Maria Dek

Princeton Architectural Press · New York

It's Sunday, and
Camille is bored.

She's read all her books, and
she's tidied her box of pencils by color.
No one is paying attention to her.

Mom reads the newspaper.

Dad folds the clothes.

Camille could just leave the house.
No one would notice.

So Camille slips quietly outside.

Outside, the sky is gray.

It's so low Camille could touch it.

Suddenly, thunder roars.

Camille shivers with happiness!

Big raindrops plop onto her head,

roll down her hair and face.

Camille sticks out her tongue:

the rain tastes like dust, like clouds.

On the ground, a column of ants zigzags and spins.

Camille watches the little red dots.

"Where are you going?" she asks.

"We're going to a show," an ant says.

"A show?"

Camille runs her hands
through the tall, wet grass.

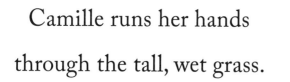

The strands tickle
her palms,

and water splashes
the tip of her nose.

She loves the plant that spreads its leaves

like an octopus in the ocean.

Camille's garden looks

like an all-green sea.

On a rosebush, beaded with rain,
a spider spins a web.
Camille studies her tangled legs
and colorful spots.

"You are too beautiful to scare me."

"I'd rather be scary," the spider says. "Hurry!

You will miss the show!"

What is this show that everyone is talking about?

Camille wonders.

Camille ponders a big tree
with powerful roots.

She imagines the roots running
deep beneath her house,
across the street, and into her
neighbor's garden.

On the ground at her feet,

Camille spots two snails,

crawling slowly.

"It's far," one said.

"It's long," the other said.

"If we had wings, we would have

been there by now."

Camille gently picks up a snail

in each hand and places them

at the foot of the tree.

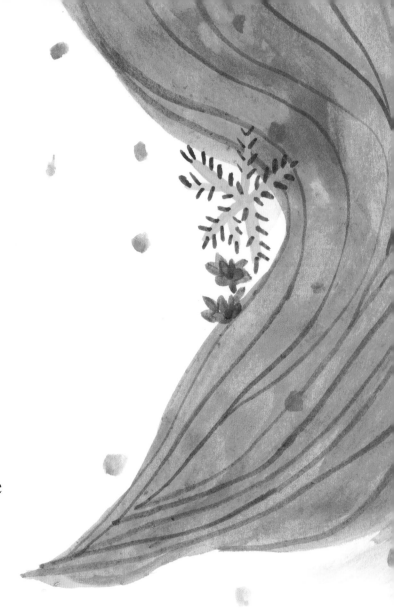

That's when Camille discovers a small, shiny black thing suspended from a branch.

"What is that?"

"It's a chrysalis,"

a bee buzzes in her ear.

Two eyes shine in the hedge.

Camille recognizes them.

They belong to the neighbor's big, gray cat.

"Look closely, Camille.

The show is about to begin!"

Suddenly, the rain stops.
A scent of damp earth and
faded flowers floats in the air.
The clouds open,
the sun begins to shine, and...

Time stops, and Camille's
heart tightens.

When she closes her eyes she can still see
the color of the new butterfly's wings
as it flies away into the bright blue sky.
It is so beautiful.

It's Sunday, and Camille

is no longer bored.

"Let's go for a walk!" Camille shouts.

"It's silly to stay inside all day."

Outside, there's always

a show to see.